Frankenstein's Monster's Kitc...

	Vials of Rat Blood			
Egg Yolk	62			

Creature Clash

Remember that once you get rid of these nice guests, you'll have to go to *727* to see what's next.

	Baroness Vamp-of-Ire	Count Vlad III Dracula	Al Phantome	Spazzombie
	711	712	713	714
Garlic	720	721	720	720
Lighter	724	720	722	728
Sword	726	722	726	723
Ghost-Hunting Permit	722	726	725	722

Question for Miss Wearywolf's Answer

If your response is . . .	What is the Earth's circumference?	What is the length of all schoolkids in the US holding hands?	What is the distance between the Earth and the moon?
Go to . . .	921	922	923

Answer to the Rat Pack's Puzzle

If you answer . . .	51	54	57
Go to . . .	931	932	933

Waking the Cursed Mirror

Golden Key	Dustcloth	Hideous Witch Mask	Mummified Hamburger
101	102	103	104

FACE CHALLENGES, ESCAPE SOLVE PUZZLES, BOOK AND ESCAPE THE BOOK!

Madam Mortell's
Haunted House

"For Nathalie . . . forever!"

Published in French under the title *Escape book –*
La maison-fantôme de Mme Hideuse
© 2019 by 404 éditions, an imprint of Édi8, Paris, France
Text © 2019 by Arthur Ténor, Illustration © 2019 by Maud Liénard

Andrews McMeel Publishing
a division of Andrews McMeel Universal
1130 Walnut Street, Kansas City, Missouri 64106
www.andrewsmcmeel.com

21 22 23 24 25 SDB 10 9 8 7 6 5 4 3 2 1

ISBN: 978-1-5248-6749-2 hardback
978-1-5248-5592-5 paperback

Library of Congress Control Number: 2020946647

Made by:
King Yip (Dongguan) Printing & Packaging Factory Ltd.
Address and location of manufacturer:
Daning Administrative District, Humen Town
Dongguan Guangdong, China 523930
1st printing—1/18/21

ATTENTION: SCHOOLS AND BUSINESSES
Andrews McMeel books are available at quantity discounts with bulk purchase for
educational, business, or sales promotional use. For information, please e-mail the
Andrews McMeel Publishing Special Sales Department:
specialsales@amuniversal.com

FACE CHALLENGES,

SOLVE PUZZLES,

AND ESCAPE THE BOOK!

Madam Mortell's Haunted House

ARTHUR TÉNOR

Andrews McMeel
PUBLISHING®

Reckless reader,

Did you know that by peeking inside this book, you've just opened the door to a new kind of attraction, a frightening journey worse than any run-of-the-mill haunted house?

You'll need your eyes, your hands, your imagination, your intelligence, and your heart. Once you've crossed the threshold and entered Madam Mortell's Haunted House, your only options will be to seek out adventure or to meet your untimely end.

Are you ready for the challenge? You should be warned: you can't even imagine the horrors in store for you! And if you really play the game, you'll be certain to have an unforgettable experience.

Good luck, poor soul!

Rules of the Game

The map of the haunted house will help you figure out where to go. As you go from room to room, you'll find objects that will come in handy later on in your adventure.

And, of course, you'll have to solve the puzzles to avoid being devoured by the other guests or find yourself stuck in a terrible place for all eternity. So focus on the instructions and the advice you're given, and don't deviate or try any funny business!

Before diving in, you should know about some important tools:

- At the end of the book, in *H1*, there's a *Horrific Adventure Notebook* where you can keep track of odds and ends.
- There are also *Horrifying Combination Tables* in *H2, or on the inside front cover*, that you should use only when you're told or when you've found the answer to a puzzle.
- You'll find some *Hints* in *H3*.
- And there are places to keep track of your *Inventory* in *H4* and *H5*.

Good luck!

There are a few things you'll have to remember.

You can go into any room from the entryway except the library. And you should know that if you don't have the right weapons or tools, things can only end badly for you. So going to the monsters' ball without having gone through the other rooms first is pretty risky—believe me. You can get to the staircase leading to the second floor only once you've found the seven code words that Madam Mortell will ask you to find. . . .

In some rooms, you'll have to grab certain *objects*—these are in *bold*. Be sure to make a note of them in your *inventory*.

In each room, you can expect to encounter someone dangerous or to undergo a challenge that will put your brain to the test. For some of them, you'll have to use the combination tables in *H2*. Each choice you make will lead you to a numbered section in the book. For example . . .

	Black Goose Quill	Letter Seal	Letter Opener
Scroll	31	32	33

If you choose to combine the scroll with the black goose quill, you then go to section *31* to see what's in store for you.

BEWARE! You can't use an object, even if it's listed in *H4*, if you haven't found it and checked it off in your inventory.

You're not allowed to cheat, for example, by reading the solution to a puzzle before trying to solve it or by walking through walls—you're not a ghost.

Just one more thing. It's about Madam Mortell, the proud owner of this extraordinary attraction. She's a very impressive woman, with her mop of red hair, a pink hairy mole on her cheek, and a large, constantly runny nose. She kinda looks like a mean old woman who likes to scare bad little children, like someone you don't want to be friends with. But enough about that! She's coming over to welcome you. *Let's hand you over to her. . . .*

Map of
Madam Mortell's House

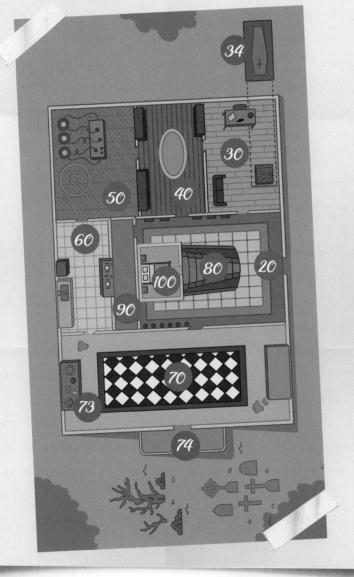

❦ Hello, Poor Soul! ❧

Oh no! What do I see here? A child! Would you like a little taste of fear to spice up your night, maybe with a pinch of horror? From your mischievous look, it's obvious you would. Your eyes are twinkling with excitement.

Besides, I'm sure you wouldn't turn down the chance to ride on an awesome ghost ride. Am I wrong? No, of course not! But will you have the guts to enter Madam Mortell's Haunted House? I guarantee you'll never be the same . . . mwahahahaha! I know, I have a hideous laugh. Normally, I use it to scare little children.

Close your eyes for a moment—just for a minute—to focus. Then picture this . . .

There's a large field on the side of a deserted road that winds through dangerous lands. It's dusk on a cold, foggy night with a full moon. You can barely see anything except for a dead tree with scary black branches. It looks like a zombie reaching out to you with its scrawny arms.

Don't get distracted. You're a curious one, aren't you? Now go down the dirt road. Oh! What is this giant shadow you suddenly see in the middle of the field? A house, a big square house. It looks like the one in *The Addams Family* with its steep, sloping black roof, its siding like an evil face. And then there are these armored skeleton statues on either side of the porch, which is covered by a worm-eaten wooden awning.

Smile, little one! You have just discovered my latest attraction. It'll make you wet your pants in fear. I call it the Haunted House! Congratulations, you have just won an infernal ride on this cursed merry-go-round.

Don't be shy. Go up to the dark door with bizarre engravings. On the left, there's a grinning old woman's face with a big mole on her cheek. That's me! If you want to find me in real life, you just have to cross this threshold. I'll be waiting for you in the hallway with a hammer. . . . No, I'm kidding! However, not just anyone can enter Madam Mortell's house. First you'll have to enter the correct code on the keypad hiding the lock.

I'll give you a hint: this trait helps me keep a haunted house that's worthy of its name.

To go look at the keypad, go to *10*.

10
The Front Door Puzzle

You have to find the right combination on this nine-digit keypad. Go look at the options in your combination tables in *H2*.

El 1	Ne 2	Tee 3
Bu 4	Zing 5	Re 6
Au 7	Tho 8	Cru 9

11

If I just teased my visitors, they would be very disappointed. To try something else, go back to *10*.

12

You've got it! Cruelty is exactly what an awful shrew like me needs to run a haunted house. You can go through to the entryway of my humble home, and we will finally be able to meet face-to-face.

To enter, go to *20*.

13

You do need authority when you have to manage a bunch of rowdy monsters. But that's not what makes me so mean. Go back to *10* and unlock this door!

14

What does that even mean? Go back to *10* and try again if you want to get in.

❧ 20 ❧
The Haunted House Entryway

Here you finally are, you little brat! I was starting to get impatient. This isn't all I've got going on, you know.

Impressive, isn't it? I think this hall is cheerfully sinister.

The drapes are moth eaten, the carpet's gone, and the chandelier is covered in cobwebs. Eek!

Listen to me carefully. And take notes if you need to.

You're standing in the entryway of my house. . . . Don't turn around! Grrr! You'll see that the door is gone and has been replaced by a portrait of my great-great-grandmother Abominannabelle.

If you're looking for an exit, the only way out is upstairs. But you can go there only after passing a few small tests.

What do I mean? It's very simple. You'll have to go through the traps . . . I mean, the *rooms* of my house . . . and find the code words that, together, will create an evil phrase that you can use to escape my haunted house.

To go search for these precious words, go look at the map of my house and pick a room.

The office of death, *30*, might be a good idea. But the ballroom, *70*, would be a very bad one. You should know that you can get to the library only through the office of death or by following my butler, Jeeves, who you'll meet eventually. So . . . hop to it!

But not so fast, little toad! Before you get started, take the time to explore the entryway. Look to your left, for example. You can see two large Chinese vases full of dead plants. *Conium maculatum*, poison hemlock, is deliciously toxic.

Between those vases, you'll see a suit of armor with a knight still inside. Ha, ha, ha! He's funny looking with his big dead grin! Did you notice his *sword*? If I were you, I'd grab it now and make a note of it in the inventory, in *H4*.

To your right is the door to the office of death, and in the corner ahead is a small round table. It is a psychic's table, used to communicate with spirits. You should notice the two objects on top of it: *a lantern* and *a lighter*, both a little old, but they do work. Go ahead and take them. They might come in handy. And be sure to make a note of them in your inventory.

Oh! Be careful! Don't move! A slithering green creature, like the color of goose poop, is approaching. It's a snake, but not just any kind; this is a prattlesnake, a species known for its talkative nature. This one's name is Slither.

Is he dangerous? Oh, no! He's just creeping under your shirt. . . . Stop squirming like that! He'll bite you! Here he is again, coming out of your collar, wrapping himself around you like a necklace and letting out a little "hiss." Now he's slithering through your hair. He finally settles on top of your head. Phew! You can breathe now. He's adopted you. From now on, he'll be there, whispering advice in your ear.

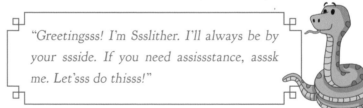

"Greetingsss! I'm Ssslither. I'll always be by your ssside. If you need assissstance, asssk me. Let'sss do thisss!"

What he means is "Pick a room." You can pick any of the rooms on the map, except the library, which you can't get to directly. To get there, you have to go through the office of death. To go to the office, go to *30*. If you'd prefer to go to the torchlit corridor, go straight to *41*.

❧ 21 ❧
Back in the Entryway

Here, you're safe from the teeth of my guests and the other terrible creatures that haunt this house—at least for the time being.

Where you go from here depends on your situation. You have two options.

If you have six code words, you're almost done! Almost—since you'll still have to solve one last little puzzle before I'll let you climb those stairs. To go work on that puzzle, go to *22*.

If you don't have all six code words, you're going to have to keep looking by going through the torchlit corridor. To go there, go to *41*. Or maybe, before that, you want to help out one of my guests who is guarding one of these treasures you so desire. To go help him, go to *22*. You can also go to *30*, to the office of death, if you haven't already been.

That makes sense, doesn't it? It's better, but you're not out of the woods just yet!

"Can you please help me?"

Oh, this skeleton looks so unhappy! He's walking toward you, but he trips with every step. Let's see what he wants.

"Wahhhh! I was visiting a mausoleum the other day, and I fell over a pile of bones and lost one of my own, my right femur. I've brought back the six bones from that pile, but since I don't have eyes, I can't figure out which one is mine! In the meantime, Madam Mortell helped me by putting a piece of wood in its place. It works, but it doesn't feel quite right. Would you be so kind, poor soul, to put my femur back in place? In exchange, I will give you a code word. How about it?"

Of course you'll do it! He puts a pile of six femurs in front of you on the tiled floor. Which is the correct one?

You can do it! Put the correct bone back where it belongs.

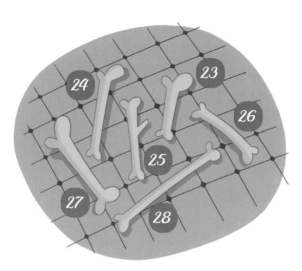

23

That's not right! Can't you tell it's a bit too short? Do you want him to be limping around?

Go back to *22* and try again.

24

That's the one! That looks like an exact copy of his left femur. The skeleton is so happy to be whole and back to perfect health—well, almost—that he gives you a bone. It's got *Odiouskulleton* written on it. Go make a note of that in your horrific adventure notebook in *H1*.

If this is the last of your seven code words, you can now go to the staircase by going to *80*.

If, on the other hand, you still have some more words to track down, you can continue exploring. Return to the entryway and go from there by going to *21*.

25

Um, no. If you compared it to his other leg, you'd see that the end of this one is smaller—not to mention that shard sticking out. If you gave him this one, he might end up losing his leg as soon as he starts moving.

Go back to *22* and try again.

26

This one has a bit too much of a curve. That would make him look a little weird.

Go back to *22* and try something else.

27

You've got to have an eye for detail for this one. On closer inspection, this femur is slightly too long. Our skeleton friend may not appreciate the joke.

Go back to *22* and try another.

 28

That's not it either! Don't you see that this femur is too long? Go back to 22 and try another one.

30
The Office of Death

You can barely see anything! To the left, there are shelves overflowing with old things, each one more disturbing than the other. My favorites are these grimacing trophies of shrunken heads and the collection of toads in jars of formaldehyde.

Oh! Someone in the room is watching you with great hunger. . . . I mean, *interest.* Look at this big desk with dragon feet carved into the legs.

It is covered by a whole bunch of objects, including an unrolled *scroll,* a sharp *letter opener* with a handle made of human bone, a *black goose quill,* but no inkwell—how weird—and *a letter seal.* . . . Make a note of these items in your inventory in *H4.*

And did you see that too? A head! The head of man, with sideburns like a 19th-century aristocrat. It looks so real you'd almost think it's alive. But it IS alive!

The chair behind the desk, which until now was facing away from you, suddenly swivels around. Oooh!

There's a body in it. It's dressed in imposing armor, and it doesn't have a head! That makes sense . . . since the head is on the desk next to him.

Who is this? Let's let him introduce himself.

"Look here, an evening visitor. Who are you, little one? Are you already tired of life? No! Don't tell me anything. I'd rather guess. Do you have any idea who I am?"

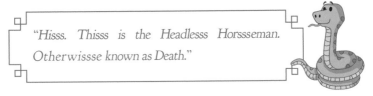

"Hisss. Thisss is the Headlesss Horsssseman. Otherwisssse known as Death."

"Are you shivering, you insignificant little human? You're right to be scared—very few leave my office alive. Come closer, so that I can better see you. Since I'm in a good mood, rather than carrying you off right away, I'm going to offer you a deal. You have everything you need on this desk to sign my contract. Then you will see what I have in store for you. A delicious, spooky surprise."

It's up to you. To sign this cursed contract, go to your combination tables in *H2*.

31

You take the quill. That's good, but there's no inkwell on the desk. To sign a contract, you need ink, or something else.

Go back to *30* and try again.

32

It is not up to you to seal this deal, but to the Headless Horseman.

Go back to *30* and try something else.

33

Well, that's an interesting idea! Since there's no inkwell on the desk but you have a quill, all you have to do is prick your finger with the letter opener.

Ouch! Of course a deal with Death can't be signed in mere ink. Go to *34* to get your spooky surprise.

𝒞 34 𝒮
Count Dracula's Tomb

As soon as you sign the contract in blood, the floor beneath your feet gives way.

Aaaah! You fall... into a tomb. You aren't badly hurt because there's a mummified corpse beneath you that cushions your fall. You hear its bones cracking as you land. Ugh! The dust! You cough, try to wave the dust out of the air, and spit the mummy dust out of your mouth. Yuck! It's gritty and gross.

Come on—get up. What do you see?

Nothing! Of course you can't see anything—you're in complete darkness. What are you going to do?

In theory, you have what you need in your inventory.

Go check your inventory and use the combination tables in *H2* to figure out what to do next.

If you don't have what you need, return to the entryway immediately by going to *20*.

341

Setting the scroll on fire will let you see around this tomb really well . . . for all of 30 seconds! And after that? Then it'll be dark again. Try something else.

Go back to *34* to try again.

342

You can make pretty sparks with a sword, but that's about it.

Go back to *34* to try again.

343

If you get attacked by an undead creature, that might come in handy. But it's not going to light up this space. How about something else?

Go back to *34* to try again.

344

Why of course! The lantern! To light it and find out what's around you, go to *35*.

✆ 35 ✆
The Tomb Puzzle

Beware! You can proceed only if you can see clearly!

With the lantern burning thanks to your lighter, you can see so much better. But what you see is not very reassuring. You seem to have landed in a burial vault. It smells musty and gross, and it's freezing cold. There's a coffin on a stone pedestal, and it looks pretty ordinary. However, its occupant doesn't seem to be, based on what's written on the lid: "Vlad III Dracula, Count of Wallachia, the Impaler" (but friends call him Dracula).

Best not disturb the coffin, in case he's in there right now. Go around this coffin carefully and examine the carved panel on the back wall.

Hmm . . . this is strange. There are five unfriendly critters carved into the panel, creatures of the night, all skillful hunters. Behind this panel is where you'll find what you're looking for. To open it, you just need to push on the right creature. But you have to figure out which one to push. I don't even want to imagine what will happen if you choose wrong.

Come a little closer to the wall and shine your light here, under the panel. It's like someone—or something—has written something in chalk . . . just before they died. Maybe that was who you landed on. This is a puzzle, an easy one to solve if you take the time to think:

"Push the creature for whom the first letter of its name is the letter of the alphabet three before the twenty-fifth."

You could do it in your sleep, you say?

Well, choose your creature, then go to the combination tables in *H2* to press on it and determine your fate.

Huh? What? Slither whispers something in your ear. A clue maybe . . .

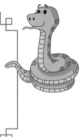

"Looksss can be dessseiving. Perhapsss the one you are looking for has another name if it'sss a different breed than the one you think. Otherwise, try using a processs of elimination. Hisss! Hisss! Hisss!"

351

The black cat? Meow! That voracious vampire cat has quite an appetite. But it's not the right creature.

Go back to *35* to try again.

352

The owl. Who! Who! Wrong one! I bet you're doing this on purpose!

Go back to *35* to try again.

353

The disgusting rat. It's way too gross. And he'll eat you up!

Go back to *35* to try again.

354

Of course it's *the bat*! The image is a vampire bat, just like Dracula. It's a bat from South America that feeds exclusively on blood. And with the twenty-fifth letter of the alphabet being Y, three letters before it is *V. V*, like vampire!

You suddenly notice a spiral staircase. You're about to get out of this sinister place. To go see what happens when you push on the bat, go to *356*.

❧ 355 ☙

You chose *the werewolf*, and someone, or something, pats you on the shoulder. You turn around.

Oh no! What big teeth he has! All the better to eat you with! What bad luck. He catches you and gobbles you up.

Go back to *35* to try again.

❧ 356 ☙

Well, Count Dracula's tomb hasn't been the most fun. At least it doesn't seem like he's here, so he won't bother you. Maybe he went to the ball. . . .

You press the vampire bat. And then . . . it's amazing! There's a click, then the sound of pulleys and old rusty gears. Finally, the panel opens, revealing a shallow compartment. Inside, you find a very old gold medallion. You grab it and read the engraving by the light of your lantern: *Traumalarkey*.

Make a note of it in your horrific adventure notebook under "code words."

You can now return to the entryway and choose a new room to go to by going to *21*, or you can go to Count Dracula's evil library by going to *40*.

40
Count Dracula's Evil Library

Beware, little one! You can go in this room
only if you've been told you can.

A library should be a pleasant place, shouldn't it? But it's much less inviting if you've been told it's evil. And yet you're going to have to go through it.

When you walk in, you notice that it's just as dark as the rest of the house. And it stinks of moldy paper.

From what you can see in the flickering light of your lantern, the shelves go from floor to ceiling and are filled with old leather-bound books. Out of curiosity, you walk over to read some of the titles: *Death Becomes Her, The Practical Guide to Hell,* by a certain Mr. Dantesque, and *Treasure Island,* by Robert Louis Stevenson. If I were you, I would take that last one and make a note of it in your inventory, just in case you end up locked in a stinky dungeon for the rest of your life.

Oh! And there, on a little shelf in the corner, do you see that thing emitting bursts of red light? A skull! It's a pirate head with a patch over the left eye, and in the other is a huge *ruby*. Go pluck it out and make a note of it in your inventory. This find will surely come in handy.

What should you do now? Should you continue between these towering shelves where you know huge black spiders will fall on you? If I were you, I'd look around a little more. You might want to go look at the map you passed when you entered the room.

> *"Hisss . . . Beware: if you take a wrong turn, you'll end up locked up in a book forever and ever!"*

What Slither means is that you should take a pencil and draw a line through the maze below WITHOUT turning around and WITHOUT ending up in a dead end. Oh, before I forget! In your harrowing journey through the maze, you'll find a *feather duster* made of harpy feathers. Pick it up and make a note of it in your inventory. That way, if you ever become Count Dracula's vampire servant, you can dust his library . . . FOREVER! Mwahahaha!

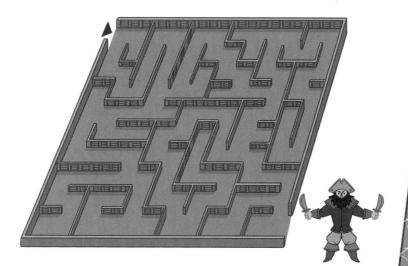

Well done! You made it out of this labyrinth of doom! But don't get too comfortable—because someone sinister is up ahead. Someone who knows no pity, no kindness, nor the fear of eternal damnation. He's even worse than me! You'll have to talk to him to get a code word. Go to 44.

41
Meet Jeeves

If you decide to explore the torchlit corridor or the art gallery, you should get shown around by a dedicated professional. I nominate . . . Jeeves!

"Come here, dear Jeeves. Please welcome our guest."

Jeeves was an exemplary butler of English aristocrats during his lifetime. Granted, his ghostly pallor makes him appear a little less fancy, but he's still a good guide, whose advice is just as reliable as Slither's.

"Hisss!"

"Sorry, dear friend. I didn't mean to upset you."

Jeeves comes forward, stiff and serious looking. He bows slightly, hands by his side. To see what happens next, go to 42, to the torchlit corridor.

42
The Torchlit Corridor

Jeeves greets you respectfully with a very pronounced British accent. "Good evening, poor soul. Please follow me. We will go through the torchlit corridor."

This is exciting, isn't it? You follow him across the entryway to the entrance of a dim and spooky corridor, where he suddenly disappears!

Don't panic. When you enter the corridor, the torches—held by real arms of flesh and bone—will light up as you pass.

Yes, Slither? You have some advice for our poor soul?

> *"Hisss! Don't go near those torchesss. They're temperamental and could reach out and ssstrangle you just for a laugh."*

You join Jeeves up ahead, stopping in front of a large closed double door. When you stick your ear to the door, you hear an orchestra playing.

Jeeves turns to you. "Here we have the ballroom. Madam Mortell gives her annual monsters' ball in there."

Would you like to enter now, or would you rather continue down the corridor to the kitchen? Let me give you some advice: if you don't have something in your inventory that will soften up the chef, you might end up tenderized and featured on today's menu.

Or you could continue toward the perilous passage . . . which is . . . well, perilous. And it could cost you an arm or even a leg. But it will lead you to Count Dracula's evil library, where you'll find a code word—that is, if you survive. But if you prefer, you can also go back to the entryway.

So, sweet poor soul, what do you choose?

To enter the ballroom—at your own risk—go to *70*. To make your way to the kitchen, go to *43*. To embark on a

treacherous journey though the perilous passage, go to *90*. Or you can return to the entryway by going back to *21*. You can use your map if you need help finding your way.

43

You choose the kitchen. Very well, but you should know that the cook is Frankenstein's monster. He's making a big pot of stew and is just waiting to have the main ingredient dropped off . . . and that ingredient is you! Mwahahaha! This is not your lucky day.

Go back to the entryway by going to *21*.

44
Captain Blackbeard

What a challenge that maze was! I hope you picked up the feather duster. I don't really know what you can use it for, but with all these dead and undead people you encounter in a haunted house . . . maybe you can use it to get rid of some of the unsightly spiderwebs.

Well, how about that! Right as you exit that maze of bookshelves, you come face-to-face with a man in an outfit that makes you think of a story you read. He's leaning against the back wall among stacks of old books. He looks like a pirate of the Caribbean. But he's not THE pirate of the Caribbean . . . he's . . .

"Blackbeard, for devil's sake!"

You might think he's a wax figure or a lifelike animatron. But it's really the REAL live Blackbeard—or at least the undead Blackbeard. And he's the victim of a curse. He's condemned to stand there, like a chained prisoner. You should go say hello.

"Hello, sir!"

"Sir?! Ha! It's been ages since I've sliced up an insolent scallywag like you. Call me Captain. You're mocking me, for skunk's sake!"

You shake your head and look terrified, because he could cut you in half, top to bottom, with that cutlass in his hand. You notice that in his other hand, he's got a sealed scroll. It must have one of those code words you're looking for.

"By my black beard, what do you want from me, matey?"

"Um . . . um . . ."

You're so intimidated that you're stammering. But you've got to do something. If he's too scary for you, you can turn around and go running and screaming. No? You want to try something else? How about you tug on his beard, laugh, and sing, "I've got your beard! I've got your beard!" Ha! Ha! Ha! Ha!

If you did that, he'd slice you right down the middle, laughing all the while. What if you questioned him politely, like the well-mannered, willing victim you are? Don't forget that he has something you want.

To talk to him, go to 45.

45

"Hello, Captain! How are you this morning? I mean, this night. . . ."

"Terrible! Can't you tell? I've been bored to death for so long in this dusty, dark place. I just want to run. I want to go back to sea by any means, for heathen's sake!"

Luckily, you forget to play dumb. "Will you please show me what you have in your hand, oh, great Captain?" you ask.

"This?" he says, raising his cutlass. "I'll make you taste it!"

You gulp, wince, and try to smile, but it comes out crooked. Then Slither whispers in your ear.

> "Captain, oh, mighty Captain, we would like to read the parchment. It'sss ssso pretty."

"Grrr! What would you trade it for?"

Quick, think! What do you have in your inventory that could be of interest to this big black-bearded brute? Go check your combination tables in *H2*, and come back here with a brilliant idea. Otherwise . . . he might just use that sword on you!

 451

Uh-oh! I think you made the wrong call.

"A rock!" Blackbeard exclaims.

"A ruby, sir—I mean, Captain," you correct yourself.

"What do you want me to do with that, for octopuses' sake!?"

And swoosh! He raises his cutlass and slices you clean down the middle.

Of course! Since he's stuck in this library, there's not much he can do with a jewel. And because you thought he'd like it, you're going to have to go get stitched back together. Lucky for you, I'm a very good seamstress.

Go back to *45* and try to make the right choice this time.

452

What a clever one you are! You use the feather duster to swipe a spider off the captain's shoulder. Well, hmm. He doesn't seem convinced. So you wave it under his nose, and he . . .

"ATCHOO!!!"

. . . sneezes hard enough to make your wig fly away. (If you had one! Ha! Ha! Ha!) Blackbeard glares at you. You'll have to try offering him something else.

Go back to *45* to try again.

453

Treasure Island! There's a brilliant idea! The captain is delighted, because he will be able to go back to the open seas and search for treasure in his imagination.

You take the scroll, unroll it, and read the code word *Landlubbereave*. Go check it off on your list.

You can now head toward Dr. Frankenstein's lab by going to *51*. Or you can go back to the entryway to choose another destination by going to *21*.

454

A lighter? Oh, sure, when he was pillaging at sea, it would surely have come in handy for lighting the wick of a cannon. But he doesn't have much use for it here.

Go back to *45* and try again.

455

You show him your sword, which provokes a violent reaction.

"Are you threatening me, you slug? Do you want me to slice open your stomach and throw your guts to the sharks just for a laugh? Ha! Ha! Ha! Ha!"

Clearly, that wasn't a good idea. Go back to *45* and try something else if you want him to lower his cutlass.

50
Dr. Frankenstein's Lab

You can enter this room only if you've been told you can.

Oh! What an oppressive atmosphere! This place looks devilishly like a lab, don't you think? But not the kind you see these days, with cold white tiles everywhere. This one's like the dark lair of a mad 19th-century scientist, just like Dr. Frankenstein, who made this horror movie monster—pretty successfully—using pieces of corpses. . . .

Oh, look! There he is, wearing his leather apron, busying himself at some sort of operating table. On it, there's a body covered in a white sheet, with large, filthy feet sticking out at one end, and at the other end . . . there's nothing.

The corpse has lost its head! And the doctor seems to have lost his mind, speaking to himself alone while scribbling in his notebook with a quill pen. And did you see his disheveled mop of hair?

You look down and notice a set of instructions on the floor. Surely, a curious kid like you can't resist. You pick up the piece of paper and see that it's a recipe, a *Halloween pancake recipe*. Have you had those yet? They're very green. Go make a note of that recipe in your inventory. Oh, and while you're at it, here's a *ghost-hunting permit*. If you meet a very mean ghost, you'll know what to do, right?

This room reeks of formaldehyde. It's filled with tubing and pipes that connect aluminum containers to larger iron ones. These are covered with gauges, metal cranks, and levers. You also see, lined up on shelves, lots of jars, some of them full of disgusting critters in a sickening yellow liquid.

And there are sounds of crackling electricity and gurgling. It's deliciously scary, isn't it?

Oh, but whom do I see coming from the back of the lab? A kind of hunched gnome with a hood and an unusual walk. He comes up and looks at you with his big, bulging eyes, like you're a tasty piece of cheese and he hasn't had lunch. His name is Igor. Be sure you pronounce it correctly or he'll bite you.

"What can I do for you, young creature?" he asks in a deeply nasal voice.

"I'd like to leave Madam Mortell's house," you reply. "A great scientist like Dr. Frankenstein must be able to help me."

"Ah, yes? Hmm, how?"

"I have no idea. Well, if . . . if he had, for example, a little code word stashed somewhere, that could help."

"A code word? You know the doctor is very busy, as you can see. He's working on his new experiment. But maybe if you help him solve a few small puzzles, he might hear you out. On the other hand, I should warn you that if you bug him for nothing, he might just make you his next guinea pig."

"Uh . . . what does that mean?"

Suddenly, the doctor exclaims, as though he'd been following the conversation, "I need a head, a nice new head!"

You gulp. You'd better hurry. . . . "OK. What are these puzzles?"

"Follow me, kind visitor."

Igor leads you to the operating table. There, he hands you a notebook with three puzzles you'll have to solve.

"Quickly, please," says Igor. "Because we don't have much time, you see."

"Logical. Everything is LO-GI-CAL! Hisss!"

Go to *52*.

Go to *52*.

⟡ 51 ⟡
Passage to
Dr. Frankenstein's Lab

Beware! You can enter only if you've been told you can.

Oh, wow! No sooner do you take the scroll from the pirate's hand than a panel opens behind him and a strong draft draws you in like a vacuum.

It messes up your hair, doesn't it? Don't worry: Slither will make sure you're presentable. You should pay more attention to what's in this large medieval-looking room you've just entered.

Go to *50* to see what I have in store for you.

❧ 52 ❧
Igor's Puzzles

Choose your answers in the combination tables in *H2*. And when you've answered all three puzzles, you can go to *53*.

1. **What word doesn't belong among these synonyms for "fear"?**

• Horror   • Alarm   • Morbid   • Dread

2. **How many graves are in the last cemetery in the series?**

3. Considering the first three skulls, what should the fourth one in the series look like?

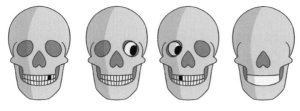

No, horror is a kind of fear. It's when you're really, really scared!

Go back to *52* and try again.

Alaaaarm! This is the kind of fear you've got when a zombie is chasing you. This isn't the word that doesn't belong.

Go back to *52* and try again.

❧ *523* ☙

Yes, since "morbid" means ghoulish or creepy and not fear like all the others.

You have solved one of the puzzles! You can go back to *52* and try the next one.

524

Aaaaah! My teeth chatter when a hungry vampire comes near because it fills me with dread, a terrible fear!

Go back to *52* and try again.

525

Um . . . I'm not following your logic.

Go back to *52* and try the second puzzle again.

526

No, that's not right. You might want to repeat your calculations.

Go back to *52* and try the second puzzle again.

527

Well done! You have solved the second puzzle! You figured out that:

0 graves in cemetery *a* + 2 graves in cemetery *b*

= 2 graves in cemetery *c*.

2 graves in cemetery *b* + 2 graves in cemetery *c*

= 4 graves in cemetery *d*.

2 graves in cemetery *c* + 4 graves in cemetery *d*

= 6 graves in cemetery *e*.

4 graves in cemetery *d* + 6 graves in cemetery *e*

= *10 graves* in the last cemetery.

Go back to *52* and try the next puzzle.

528

Your own skull is going to end up on Dr. Frankenstein's shelf if you don't get this right!

Go back to *52* and try the third puzzle again.

529

You got it! Do you need it explained? No? Well, I'll tell you anyway. You add up the differences in each skull to get the last.

For the eyes:

0 + 1 + 1 = 2 eyeballs—one in each socket

For the missing teeth:

1 + 0 + 1 = 2 missing teeth

If you've solved all three of Igor's puzzles, go to 53.

530

That could have been it, but it's not. Think a little harder.

Go back to *52* and try the third puzzle again.

You have solved the puzzles and earned the right to bother the mad scientist.

"Excuse me, doctor. Can I ask you for a favor?"

"What now?!" he yells.

You jump but then manage to pull yourself together. And that's a good thing, because this guy is ready to tear you apart—starting with that pretty little head of yours.

"The code word—could I have it?" you ask.

"*Rapidlythal!* Igor, bring me a full head!"

Well, there you have it! Your word! Not an easy one to pronounce.

Quickly make a note of it on your list, then get out before Igor considers your head for his master's needs.

You can go to *60*, to Frankenstein's monster's kitchen. Or if you're not hungry, you can go back to the entryway by going to *21*.

60
Frankenstein's Monster's Kitchen

Beware, poor soul: if you enter this place without anything
to satisfy the cook, things might get quite dicey.

The room you are about to enter might allow you to get a
code word and enter the ballroom, where there's a fiendish
party going on. You might also find one or two useful things
to add to your inventory.

On the other hand, you could leave behind an arm, or a
leg, or a head, or even your whole body if you don't manage
to win over the chef.

Just a note: This is Dr. Frankenstein's monster. He's not
a big talker, but he makes a killer crusted brat-wurst and a
tasty kid kebab. You've got this! Push open this swing door
and try to cross the room discreetly by going to *61*.

61

You're in Frankenstein's monster's kitchen, which is actually kind
of normal looking, at least for a kitchen from the 19th century.

On the long oak table, you see a bowl full of appealing—
but poisoned—fruit and a plate of candied witches' fingers
ready to be taken to the ball's buffet.

Be very careful and put this *clove of garlic* in your inventory. It's quite effective at repelling certain night predators. There are also some knives, an eye, and an ear here and there. Nothing out of the ordinary.

But you'll want to pay special attention to the jars of various ingredients and colored spices lined up on the table.

Near the wall, to your right, there's a wood stove, one a master chef might have used long ago. It looks like someone is frying up viper tongues and ostrich-eye donuts in a big black pan. It's the cook!

Eek! He's a mass of muscle, this guy. Eight feet tall. Shoulders like a bull.

He's wearing a hat that's way too small for his square head. . . . Oh! He must have heard you because he's turning around. The stunning monstrosity before you makes you yell so loud your jaw nearly comes loose. Then he smiles with all his rotten teeth. What a mug!

He seems happy that you're here. But beware—this could be because this cook loves children . . . in a stew.

"Gromf! Eugreuu, gragrew!"

(Approximate translation: "Welcome to my humble laboratory of sweets to be enjoyed with friends on nights with a full moon.")

"Rrrrah! Gromf! Grongrongnonmf!"

("Can I invite you to join me at the table? Our guests' table . . . Ha! Ha! Ha!")

In other words, he wants to put you on today's menu.

Of course, you're not excited about this idea. But to escape the cleaver, I think you'll have to do something to make him happy, for example, demonstrating your culinary talents.

If you look in your inventory, you should find something that will help you, especially if you came through Dr. Frankenstein's lab.

Otherwise, you might want to go back to the entryway by returning to *21* or to the office of death by going to *30*.

If, on the other hand, you think you have what you need to make this ugly cook happy, then go get to work by going to *67*.

62

Rat's blood is red. If you mix the vial of rat blood with yellow, you'll have orange pancakes, not green. Gross!

Go back to 67 and try something else.

63

The powdered mummy pee is yellow. It won't make your pancakes green.

Try again. And be quick, because Frankenstein's monster is already growling. You don't have long before you end up on his menu.

Go back to 67 and try something else.

64

Let's try this and see what happens. The blueberry elixir mixed with the egg yolk makes . . . yes! Well done! What a beautiful green batter! The cook is so delighted that he forgets all about you and goes to fry them up.

You're about to take this opportunity to slip away to the ballroom when Slither whispers in your ear.

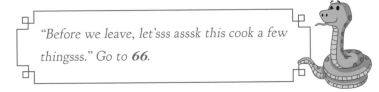

"Before we leave, let'sss asssk this cook a few thingsss." Go to **66**.

65

Widows' tears are salty, and a little salt is good in pancakes, but purple mixed with the yellow egg yolk won't make your pancakes green.

Go back to *67* and try again.

66

"Excuse me, but is there any chance you know a code word?"

He turns around, looking grumpy. Don't panic; that's the way he always looks.

"Gronf! *Loonyscattacker*," he answers.

"Thank you!"

Go make a note of the word in your horrific adventure notebook.

If you've got all the items checked off in your inventory, then you can go to *70*. If not, there are some rooms you still need to visit. Go back to the entryway to continue exploring by going to *21*.

67

You've got that recipe for Halloween pancakes in your inventory. That's perfect. You've got everything you need on the kitchen table to make some good pancakes. But they've got to be green. Darn! None of the colorful spices you see are green.

Which one of these should you choose? Go to your combination tables in *H2* to try mixing some of these ingredients.

Before you go, though, you should listen to Slither's advice.

"Hisss! There are bird eggsss there. They have the tastiessst yellow yolksss."

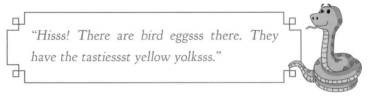

◦ 70 ◦
The Monsters' Ballroom

Beware! Not just anyone can enter here. You have to have something in your inventory that you can use to defend yourself from this spooky ball's most dangerous guests. If you don't, you might just meet your end!

My, my! Just look at this place! The band of the living dead at the far end of the ballroom plays a frenzied ghoulish polka. The decor is nice, with grand cobwebs in the chandeliers and critters everywhere: hairy tarantulas climbing the drapes, rats running along the walls, black cats clawing on the moth-eaten velour curtains. . . .

And what a show these dancing couples are putting on! A werewolf looking as serious as a heart attack, zombies

devouring their eyeballs, mummies stepping on their own wrappings as they dance. . . . There's even a zombie courting a charming ghoul who smells of a putrid marsh. On your right, there's a sumptuous buffet of delicacies for the guests. You might go over there soon to check it out yourself.

Until then, find yourself a quiet corner and take a seat . . . such as on this stool where an executioner has left a severed head. You can take the seat after cautiously kicking it off.

If you are asked to dance, or just chat, you should think about it for a second before saying yes—because you're not here for fun; you're here to find a code word. Either you can search the room for it and risk drawing attention to yourself—and given who's in this room, I wouldn't recommend that—or you could try to question these distinguished guests. I'm sure they all know the answer, and if you chat with some of them, they'll undoubtedly drop hints as to where and how to find your code word. When you have all the details you need, make certain you take plenty of notes in your horrific adventure notebook in *H1*.

Go to *71* to see what happens next.

❧ 71 ❧

What bad luck! You've already been spotted, and, in this group, any interaction could end badly. Don't panic. Go check your inventory and see whether you have something you can use to get rid of anyone who wants to get acquainted.

After each meeting, you'll have to go look at your combination tables in *H2* and choose which way you'll try to escape my guests' appetites. Oh! I'd better make myself scarce. One of them is coming this way now. . . .

Go to *711*.

❧ 711 ❧

It's a pale lady with dark purple circles under her eyes. I don't want to make fun, but she might want to rethink that ridiculous beehive hairstyle. A huge spider has even made itself a home in it. And have you seen how worn out her dress is? I bet she's undead . . . but very lively! Just look at how her arms and legs are waving around like a double-jointed puppet. Oh, shhhhh! She's coming. . . .

"Hello, you! Hello, hello!" she says, unfolding her fan, which has only slats left. "Would you like to dance with the Baroness Vamp-of-Ire?"

Of course, you accept her macabre invitation.

"La la-laaaa! La, la-laaaa! La-la-la, la-la-la, la-la-la," she hums a Viennese waltz while spinning among the other dancers.

Considering your greenish complexion, it looks like you might be getting seasick.

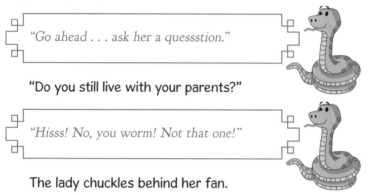

"Go ahead . . . ask her a quessstion."

"Do you still live with your parents?"

"Hisss! No, you worm! Not that one!"

The lady chuckles behind her fan.

You try something else, but your shyness makes you start babbling. "You're so very . . . old. I mean, gold! You're as, um . . . precious as gold! Agh!"

"Oh, thank you! How charming. No one has given me such a compliment since . . . oooh! The last witch and ghost party I attended. Do you know the one? What was that called again? It's terrible how you start to lose your memory when you get to be 250 years old. It rhymes with creak, like my knees."

If I were you, I'd try to get away while you can. It won't be long before she starts looking at you as less of a dance partner and more of a dessert. . . . Do you have anything you can use to defend yourself? Go to your creature clash

combination table in *H2* to figure out your escape and see who you'll talk to next.

✿ 712 ✿

Oh, look. There's an elegant aristocrat observing the dancers while drinking from a cup of fresh blood with a straw. Go and introduce yourself.

"Good evening, sir! I am Madam Mortell's . . . guest. And you are?"

He looks at you and raises an eyebrow. "'Sir'? You don't say. Those who know me actually call me 'Master' or 'Count.' Count Vlad III Dracula, at your service. . . . Now, now, don't make that face. You look like a jack-o'-lantern that's bitten into a lemon. But I do have to say . . . you have a lovely neck, with a beautiful . . . jugular vein."

Wasn't he just sleeping in his tomb? If that wasn't him, then maybe it was his brother. Either way, this guy's got magnificent canines.

You'll want to get away quickly before this charming vampire abandons his cup of AB+ to try your blood type. But escaping Dracula's voracious thirst is impossible. That is, unless you have something that will repel him.

Go to your creature clash combination table in *H2* to figure out how you're going to escape.

ᘒ 713 ᘓ

You come across a new creature, Al Phantome. This one shouldn't be too hard to handle. But beware—this ghost was a mobster when he was alive.

"Oh, look, a lost little mortal."

"No, no, actually, I'm looking for . . ."

"A nice little chat with someone who will give you the code word to get you out of here? Look no further; I'm your man. Or, I was. As you can see, I don't have a body anymore. Follow me! It's at the buffet."

I think this guy's told you enough. Go to your creature clash combination table in *H2* to figure out how you're going to get away from him.

ᘒ 714 ᘓ

Ouch! A brute grabs your arm and spins you around. By all that's unholy, he's an ugly one! A zombie!

"Good evening, my name is Zany Spazzombie. I'll buy that from you! Name your price."

"Buy what?"

"Your sword. It would be so efficient at splitting heads open to eat the brains."

Gulp. You have to get away from this guy as quickly as possible!

Go to your creature clash combination table in *H2* to figure out how you're going to escape.

720

Yeah, OK. I'm not sure that's enough to make this creature turn and run. It might have something to do with not having a nose anymore.

Go back to your creature clash table in *H2* and try again.

721

You take a big clove of garlic out of your pocket. Your opponent's eyes widen in terror.

Chomp! You bite right into the garlic. Mmm, the breath it gives you . . . The vampire squeals and runs away, flailing his arms. So, Dracula, looks like you lost this round.

Have you met everyone who's listed in your creature clash table yet? If not, go to *H2* and pick someone else, then go to *713* or *714*. If you've met and defeated them all, go to *727*.

722

Ha! Like that's going to work! Your opponent laughs at you and . . . chomp! What a sad ending for you.

Go back to your creature clash table in *H2* and try again.

723

That's not a bad idea. You take your sword and cut off the beast's head! What a sight to see this poor, cursed creature running after its head like a dog chasing a ball.

The problem is that you're dealing with an undead creature who doesn't need a head to continue dancing . . . and cutting off a creature's head is not a good way to make friends. You find yourself grabbed by the neck and having the life squeezed out of you.

Go back to your creature clash table in *H2* and try again.

724

Yes! Of course! The lighter works on anyone who hates fire.

There's a lock of the baroness's hair that's fallen to her shoulder and looks just like a stick of dynamite. It's too tempting. You set fire to it with your lighter.

The flames make her panic. You use the opportunity to escape and find another dance partner. Are there any you haven't scared off yet?

Go back to your creature clash table in *H2* and pick someone else, then go to *712*, *713*, or *714*.

725

You had to think about that one, didn't you? You wave your ghost-hunting permit under his nose. It must bring back bad memories, because he suddenly bolts like he's running from the ghost cops.

Well done! You can go to *727*. That is, unless there are some creatures you haven't interacted with yet. In which case, go back to your creature clash table in *H2* and pick someone else, then go to *712* or *714*.

726

Nope. That doesn't work. But at least nothing bad happened. Because who knows. Any choice could kill you! Mwahahaha!

Go back to your creature clash table in *H2* and try again.

727

What clues did you gather during your conversations?

I hope you took good notes in your horrific adventure notebook in *H1*. If you have, you should know where to go.

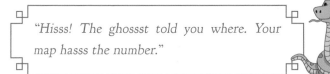

> "Hisss! The ghossst told you where. Your map hasss the number."

Still stuck? Need a hint? Go to *H3*.

728

You wave your lighter under what was once a nose. He eyes it with a questioning look, then suddenly seems to understand. This creature hates fire. He turns and runs, flailing his arms like an exhausted orangutan.

Have you met everyone in your creature clash table yet? If not, go to *H2* and pick someone else, then go to *712* or *713*. If you've met and defeated them all, go to *727*.

73
The Buffet of Horrors

Not to brag, but I take care of my guests. There's something for everyone here: exotic-blood cocktails, slug liver toast, an assortment of tied tongues, horsefly guts, newborn-bird dropping mousse, bite-size earwax cakes. . . .

Look at what's in front of you. Among all these horrific delicacies, a few deserve special attention because one of them is hiding a code word.

Is it in this *laughing head of a madman* pickled with sock juice? In this *zombie skull* preserved in stomach acid? Or in this *haunted house cake* made of pine bread? (When you peek under the roof, you'll find it filled with grilled rat guts. They taste kind of like crispy earthworms.) Or could it be under the *top hat*, filled with green mice that you can dip in elbow grease and stagnant swamp water, before swallowing them whole? Or could it be in this beautiful grimacing *jack-o'-lantern*?

All this is making you hungry, I know. But you've got to think about what you need to do to find that code word. Look in your inventory to see whether you have anything that could help you.

Think about what clues the creatures you've talked with have given you. If you think hard, you'll know what item on the buffet to choose and what you have to do with it.

And you took good notes in that horrific adventure notebook, right?

 731

LAUGHING HEAD OF A MADMAN

You split it in half while laughing your own head off. It's a lot of fun, but it has nothing to do with the clues you've been given.

Go back to 73 and try again.

 732

HAUNTED HOUSE CAKE

Yum! These grilled rat guts are delicious. You rummage around in there and spill everything on the table . . . but you don't find any code word. Were you even listening for clues?

Go back to 73 and try again.

733

ZOMBIE SKULL

You take your sword and lop off the top of the skull, just like a boiled egg. Inside, it looks just like you'd expect a 100-year-old boiled egg to look. And it smells even worse! Of course, there's no code word.

Go back to 73 and try again.

❧ 734 ❧

JACK-O'-LANTERN

Holy demons! Of course! You split it open with a single stroke of your sword, and its orange brains spill out onto the buffet table. In the middle of this carnage, you find a small skull with *Exquisitleaches* engraved on it. Make a note of this word in your horrific adventure notebook in *H1*, then escape this place via the balcony by going to *74*.

❧ 735 ❧

TOP HAT

Stabbing water would have had more of an impact. Why did you choose this? I guess we'll never know.

You'll have to go back to *73* and find something else to use that sword on.

74
The Balcony

Your stroke of brilliance, or rather the strike of your sword, doesn't go unnoticed. The band suddenly stops, and in that deadly silence, all eyes, including the skeletons' empty sockets, turn your way. Uh-oh! It looks like there's about to be a feeding frenzy. If I were you, I would make my way out of here quietly.

Your only escape is through the glass door to the balcony. Luckily, it's wide open. If you get that far, you don't have any other option. You'll have to jump over the stone railing, hope you haven't broken any bones, then run.

Are you ready? Frankenstein's monster is coming out of his kitchen brandishing a meat cleaver that looks freshly used.

"Rrraah!"

He's going to get you! Run, little toad, run quickly! It's your only hope! And if you manage to escape, go to *741*.

741

You run until you're out of breath, which is a good thing, because you've got a whole bunch of creatures just behind you and they are as cursed as they are hungry. In the dark and fog, you can't really take the time to enjoy your surroundings, which is too bad, because you just saw a very nice cemetery. Maybe you should go hide there. My great-grandmother Dummartha's tomb has a secret passage that will bring you directly to the entryway. You'll recognize it easily. It's a stone structure with a guillotine at the entrance. If you run through it fast enough, you might not lose your head. Mwahahaha!

And that's how, like in the worst nightmares, you end up right back at the entryway. And you should know that, even though you were just outside, you can now escape my house only by going upstairs. . . .

"Aaaah!"

Yes, yes, hurry. They're coming. And they look murderous.

Go to *21*.

❧ 80 ❧
The Staircase

Beware! You can climb this staircase only if you have the seven haunted house code words. Do you? Then you can go home! But not before one last little challenge.

If you're missing a word, maybe you haven't helped out one of my guests—the one in the hallway. Go back to *21*, get your last code word, and come back here quickly!

Jeeves gestures to the stairs. "Please follow me, if you don't mind. Take care—these steps are treacherous."

He's not kidding. This staircase is very old. It's worm eaten and full of traps for poor souls. Each step has a truly bizarre inscription. You ask Jeeves whether he can explain.

He replies, "Best to know where you set foot when you risk going upstairs in Madam Mortell's Haunted House. There's a rumor that one of the steps is a hiding place for a treasure that might allow you to fly the coop, if you know what I mean."

I hope you do. If you don't, you're never getting out of here.

"Is that so? And which step is it?"

"One that won't eat your arm or leg or that's not empty. Do you still want to go up, poor soul?"

Seeing his little pinched smile, you can tell he's trying not to sneer at the thought of you setting foot on the wrong step.

Take a good look at this staircase by the light of your lantern and be careful. Some steps will easily support your weight. Others will not, and you're guaranteed to fall. Some are a real trap, while others are neither dangerous nor useful. You should be aware that your legs are not long enough to take more than two steps at a time. One last piece of advice: Don't trust the order of the step numbers. But pay attention to the words written on them. And, of course, you go up a staircase by starting at the bottom. You're no bat, are you?

800

This step looks clear. . . . It looks like you're safe.

Follow Jeeves to a new room by going to *100*.

801

Maybe this is the right step . . . because you can lift it like a hatch. You bend over and shine your light inside . . . EMPTY! Well, almost. A huge black spider has made himself at home in here. Since this step is harmless, you can close it quickly and keep heading up by going to *809* or *806*.

802

Not this one! You poor thing! No sooner have you set foot on it than two skeletal hands come out of two small hatches and grab your ankle. Fortunately, you have what you need to set yourself free. In two strikes of your sword, you get rid of those clingy hands. But you lose your balance and fall.

Go back to *80*.

803

Look at this . . . . You can open up this step. It's a good place for *Madam Mortell's Hidden TREASURE*. It's filled with all kinds of things, some of which will help you leave the haunted house. You take a *golden key*, a *dustcloth*, a *hideous witch mask*, and an incredibly unappetizing *mummified hamburger*. Check all these off in the list of *Madam Mortell's Hidden Treasure* in *H5* and keep heading up the stairs by going to *805* or *807*.

804

You hear a sinister creak. Do you keep going?

It's too WEAK. The step breaks like a rotten plank, and your leg sinks in. What if there's a swarm of rats under there ready to feast on you? Gulp!

Go back down to *80* quickly if you want to keep both your feet.

805

It's a TRAP! Your leg sinks into the step, and you tumble down the stairs.

Go back down to *80* and start again, if you ever want to get out of here.

806

At least this one doesn't break on you. It's SOLID! You can keep heading up the stairs by going to *804* or *803*.

807

At least this one doesn't break on you. It's SOLID! You can get to the landing by stepping on the next step, which is clear. Phew! You're almost out of danger.

Follow Jeeves to a new room by going to *100*.

808

There's nothing to worry about here. This step looks rather SOLID.

Go to the next one, either *802* or *801*.

809

Ooh, bad choice! This step is very unstable. You slip and go flying backward, waving your arms as you tumble all the way down.

Go back to *80* and try again.

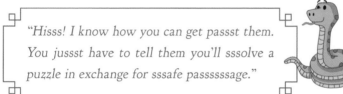

This choice is a wise one, that is, if you manage not to get devoured by Miss Wearywolf, or be drained of your blood by Madam Leechbottom, or have your feet chewed on by the Rat Pack.

> *"Hisss! I know how you can get passst them. You jussst have to tell them you'll sssolve a puzzle in exchange for sssafe passssssage."*

If Miss Wearywolf is blocking your path, you can offer to find the question to her answer. She loves that game. If you can figure out the question, you'll be able to pass. If you don't . . . you pass away. Mwahahaha!

Madam Leechbottom likes puzzles too. She'll ask you to solve one. If you do, you can sneak past her. If you don't . . . slurp! She'll drink every last drop of your blood.

As for the Rat Pack, they'll give you a math puzzle. Nothing very complicated. But if you lose count, you might lose a toe or two.

Enter the perilous passage by going to *91*.

91

You enter the dark tunnel, your little heart tight with fear. I hope that you have something to light your way, or you won't even see your end coming.

The floor is spongy, and there are big patches of slime you have to get around.

It seems like you're walking through a smelly swamp. . . . Oh! There's a tall, pale figure ahead, dripping murky water. It's Madam Leechbottom, and she's got a puzzle for you. She's a truly repulsive sight to behold, and her teeth will send shivers down your spine. I hope for your sake that the puzzle won't be too hard.

Jeeves asks you, "Have you made a note of your answer in your horrific adventure notebook? Very good. Let us continue, if you don't mind."

Beware! You can go to *92* only if you've managed to solve Madam Leechbottom's puzzle. If you've tried but you can't figure it out, go to *H3* to get some help.

 92

Jeeves leads you down what seems to be a grassy path through the woods. Something doesn't feel quite right, and you have your suspicions confirmed when you hear a bloodcurdling wolf howl. You stop dead in your tracks as something brushes your shoulder. You spin around . . . . Eeeeeee! You're facing a huge wolf. It's Miss Wearywolf. Quick! Challenge her to a game before she bites off your head.

"Good evening, Miss Wearywolf. You have an answer for me, I believe."

"Grrr! I do. How about this: 238,900 miles."

Easy. Go make your choice in the combination tables in *H2*. Then you can go where the table tells you.

But before that, Slither has a clue for you.

"It'sss what ssseparatesss one from the other. Missssss Wearywolf goesss out only when you can sssee all of one. And she alwaysss keepsss her pawsss on the other."

921

That's not it! That's 24,901 miles!

Go back to **92** and try again.

922

Wrong! There are 56.6 million schoolkids in the US. Even if we use three feet per kid, that would only be 32,159 miles.

Go back to **92** and try again.

923

Well done! Since Miss Wearywolf has no more reason to devour you, go to **93**.

❧ 93 ❧

The Rat Pack is waiting for you a little farther down the passage, where it turns into a dark and narrow tunnel again.

In order for them to let you pass, you'll have to solve the following little problem in your head: *If six raccoons each make three black masks in five minutes, how many will they all make in 15 minutes?* Go check your answer in your combination tables in *H2*.

❧ 931 ❧

17 × 3. No, you've miscalculated it.

Go back to *93* and try again.

❧ 932 ❧

That's right! It's 18 × 3.

Go to *94*.

❧ 933 ❧

That would be what you'd get if you'd done 19 × 3, but that's not quite right.

Go back to *93* and try again.

94

The perilous passage leads to the art gallery.

You've done well, it seems, since you're still here in one piece. Maybe my butler can share some secrets with you. . . .

"Jeeves, do you know of a code word that's whispered between poor souls when they meet?"

"Certainly: Murmurder."

Murmurder is right! You never know what's around any corner!

You can now go to the library by passing through the entryway by going to *40*.

However, if you've already found seven code words and you've listed them in your notebook, you can try to get upstairs by going to *80*.

100
The Room of
Madam Idiotilda's Cursed Mirror

Jeeves, stoic and stiff as always, says, "If you'd kindly enter here, you are expected."

"Is that so? Who's expecting me?"

"Alas, poor soul! You will have to leave us . . . feetfirst

or headfirst, depending on your speech. Break a leg, as my mistress would say."

Hopefully, luck be on your side. Let's not put this off any longer. You cross the dusty corridor, and Jeeves opens the door to what was once the bedroom of my great-aunt Idiotilda! She was so pimply and slimy—and she gave kisses like a slug. It was horrible . . . but I digress. What do you see in here?

For now, by the light of your lantern, through swirls of dust, you see a canopy bed on the right and a chest of drawers covered with old photos of mummy, vampire, and zombie family members on the left. Oh, and there's a big mirror, there! It's a full-length oval mirror that would delight any antiques dealer. Approach carefully—it's cursed. What does that mean, you ask?

Jeeves explains, "It is said that, in the late Miss Idiotilda's time—that's the great-aunt of our mistress—this mirror was a passage."

"A passage to what?" you ask.

"Well, it depends. If you pronounce the right phrase correctly, you leave this haunted house by the shortest route. If you are mistaken, you descend straight to a realm of eternal torment and suffering."

Mwahahaha! I find this terribly amusing—don't you?

This is the moment of truth for you. Allow me to summarize: To get through the cursed mirror, you have to pronounce a magic phrase. Then you will either descend to the abyss or go back home. The problem is that this dusty, spotted old mirror has been dormant for quite some time. *So you have to start by waking it up.* Go look at the odds and ends you stole from my hiding place in the staircase, then go to *H2* to see whether you can use anything to wake this mirror up. His name is Mirroricio.

101

You don't have a door with a lock in front of you. You have a mirror. Keep going like this and I'll keep you . . . forever! Mwahahaha!

Go back to *100* and try again.

102

Try and see. Ooooh! By removing this thick layer of dust, you have restored Mirroricio's luster. He's so happy that he stops staring at you.

Go to *105* to see what happens next.

103

My great-aunt made that face when she wanted to make little kids scream. And you scream when you see yourself in Mirroricio, then you run away, calling out for help. It's a shame. I'm going to have to keep you . . . forever. Unless you come up with a better idea.

To try something else, go back to *100*.

104

And why not roasted ham and butter?! Start over, before I get mad. Go back to *100*.

105
The Spell to Make You Pull Out Your Hair

Finally, Mirroricio deigns to open an eye. His ghostly face looks like he ate something that disagreed with him, and it's not pretty. But you will have to be OK with it, and you'll have to listen to him.

"Hello, you. How can I thank you for waking me up in the middle of a nightmare? I saw myself seeing myself, seeing myself, seeing myself, seeing myself—"

"By telling me how can I get home."

It was a good thing you interrupted him because he could have gone on like that for a century.

"How? You know how. You have to say your code words IN THE RIGHT ORDER! Otherwise, I'll send you straight to Hades."

"Oh? What's Hades like?"

"Ha! It's full of children sitting at their desks. They have to do their homework forever and ever, and if they ever stop, demons armed with rulers whack their knuckles so that they get back to work."

Slither has a clue to help you find the right order. Don't you, Slither?

"Hisss! I was dreaming of apples. OK, yesss, a clue for the end. If you hide usss, we're in the wrong order. Put everything in the right order and you'll win."

Go to your horrific adventure notebook in *H1* to see the possible combinations.

106

MET ROLL. I would be surprised if that worked.

Go back to *H1* and try again.

107

TROLL ME. Yeah, that's bad. I don't think that's it. Got another idea?

Go back to *H1* and try again.

108

MORTELL. What a good idea to order the code words so the first letters spell out my pretty name. This deserves a reward.

Go to *109*.

109

Here's what you have to do: Go stand in front of Mirroricio, then say the phrase loudly and without stuttering. Take your time. Practice. And when you feel ready and confident . . . go for it! When you can say it, you'll be able to get out!

Go to the epilogue.

❧ Epilogue ☙

Oh my word, what an adventure!

I hope you peed your pants. You didn't? Either way, you're not about to forget it. Because that would be a shame, wouldn't it, Jeeves?

"Certainly, Madam Mortell. But I intend to remain in the service of our poor soul until the end of their life."

"What do you mean?"

"While they sleep, I will be at their beck and call, especially if they have delicious nightmares. I will be a ghost butler worthy of my name!"

And you, Slither, do you intend to stay in our young guest's hair for long?

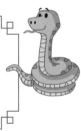

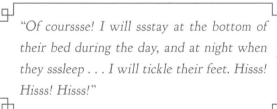

"Of courssse! I will ssstay at the bottom of their bed during the day, and at night when they sssleep . . . I will tickle their feet. Hisss! Hisss! Hisss!"

Well, then, it's time to say farewell . . . or fare terribly, as I like to say.

"Hey, hey, hey! I have something to say too!"

Yes, Count Dracula?

"Everyone knows that I am a creature of the night. And that I love night parties, especially Halloween nights. I would like to invite our dear little friend back to our monsters' ball every year."

You accept, of course.

"Can I say something too?"

Mr. Zany! What do you want?

"I want to say goodbye to our visitor . . . and I'd like to invite them to come back to Madam Mortell's Haunted House to see us. And to bring friends. We can all have fun!"

That we can!

Thank you very much, dear readers and spectators. Madam Mortell's Haunted House will now have a change of scenery. But it will always be here for you!

Mwahahaha!

Your Horrific Adventure Notebook

What You Learn from Your Encounters at the Monsters' Ball
Check off the creatures you manage to fend off at the ball, and write down the hints they give you. These will lead you to the ballroom code word.

☐ Baroness Vamp-of-Ire . . . .

☐ Count Vlad III . . . .

☐ Al Phantome . . . .

☐ Spazzombie . . . .

You've got all the details you need to continue your quest, don't you? You must have learned WHERE to go to find your code word. If you're struggling and need some help, go to 727.

You also know WHAT to do once you get there. But if you're not too sure and want to double-check, go to *H3* for a hint. But you should go there only if you're still stuck after going to 727!

Answers for the Perilous Passage Puzzles

- Write the answer to Madam Leechbottom's puzzle below.
  What do you think it means? If you need some help, go to
  H3 for a hint.

....

Code Words

1 ☐ Traumalarkey
2 ☐ Landlubbereave
3 ☐ Rapidlythal
4 ☐ Odiouskulleton
5 ☐ Loonyscattacker
6 ☐ Exquisitleaches
7 ☐ Murmurder

And if you put them in the right order, what do you get?

If you think it's this . . .	7-6-1-3-4-2-5	1-3-4-2-5-7-6	7-4-3-1-6-2-5
Go here . . .	106	107	108

Horrifying Combination Tables

Combinations

The Front Door Puzzle

3-5	9-1-3	7-8-6-3	9-5
11	12	13	14

The Office of Death Puzzle

	Black Goose Quill	Letter Seal	Letter Opener
Scroll	31	32	33

Count Dracula's Tomb

	Scroll	Sword	Letter Opener	Lantern
Lighter	341	342	343	344

The Tomb Puzzle

The Black Cat	The Owl	The Disgusting Rat	The Bat	The Werewolf
351	352	353	354	355

The Blackbeard Puzzle

	Ruby	Feather Duster	*Treasure Island*	Lighter	Sword
Captain	451	452	453	454	455

Igor's Puzzles

1. **What word doesn't belong among these synonyms for "fear"?**

Horror	Alarm	Morbid	Dread
521	522	523	524

2. **How many graves are in the last cemetery in the series?**

	14 Graves	9 Graves	10 Graves
Cemetery	525	526	527

3. **Considering the first three skulls, what should the fourth one in the series look like?**

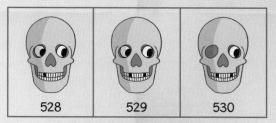

| 528 | 529 | 530 |

Frankenstein's Monster's Kitchen Puzzle

	Vials of Rat Blood	Powdered Mummy Pee	Toxic Blueberry Elixir	Purple Widows' Tears
Egg Yolk	62	63	64	65

Creature Clash

Remember that once you get rid of these nice guests, you'll have to go to 727 to see what's next.

	Baroness Vamp-of-Ire	Count Vlad III Dracula	Al Phantome	Spazzombie
	711	712	713	714
Garlic	720	721	720	720
Lighter	724	720	722	728
Sword	726	722	726	723
Ghost-Hunting Permit	722	726	725	722

Question for Miss Wearywolf's Answer

If your response is . . .	What is the Earth's circumference?	What is the length of all schoolkids in the US holding hands?	What is the distance between the Earth and the moon?
Go to . . .	921	922	923

Answer to the Rat Pack's Puzzle

If you answer ...	51	54	57
Go to ...	931	932	933

Waking the Cursed Mirror

Golden Key	Dustcloth	Hideous Witch Mask	Mummified Hamburger
101	102	103	104

H3
Hints

The Ballroom Puzzle

(Where should you look for your code word?)

If you paid close attention to the conversations you had in the ballroom, you might remember that the mobster ghost was trying to lead you to the buffet of horrors. You can get there by going to 73.

Madam Leechbottom's Puzzle in the Perilous Passage

Madam Leechbottom's puzzle: eye, heart, two swamps, a knot, two cemeteries. She's saying, "I love swamps, not cemeteries."

If you got it right, which I'm sure you did, you can get your code word by going to 92.

H4
Your Inventory

Check the items you found:

☐ Lantern ☐ Letter seal

☐ Halloween pancake recipe ☐ Feather duster

☐ Lighter ☐ Letter opener

☐ Clove of garlic ☐ *Treasure Island*

☐ Sword ☐ Scroll

☐ Black goose quill ☐ Ghost-hunting permit

☐ Ruby

H5
Madam Mortell's
Hidden Treasure

☐ Golden key

☐ Dustcloth

☐ Hideous witch mask

☐ Mummified hamburger

Map of
Madam Mortell's House